Little Sunflower

By Sarah Gilbert

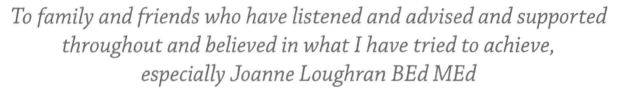

To family and friends who have listened and advised and supported throughout and believed in what I have tried to achieve, especially Joanne Loughran BEd MEd

To Thomas ...... as mentioned before ... who is the best wee man in the world.

Lucas

By Sarah Gilbert

Illustrated by JJ Quinlan

Little Sunflow

strong and he knew that he was.

He felt good. He also felt that he was different.

were smaller than him.

Sometimes they looked at him with big wide frightened eyes. Just like little Milo Mouse over there.

He glanced back at the little mouse. Milo Mouse
was trying his best to look brave over in the corner.

He wondered why he was so frightened. Lucas
Lion was used to being talked about and his strength
was admired all the time.

looked like that. And he never felt cautious or nervous.

Lucas Lion held his head up high. He opened his large mouth and let out a mighty roar!

The leaves on the Little Sunflower fluttered and the stem tilted sideways with the force of his breath.

'Oh', thought the Little Sunflower, 'Lucas Lion is so big and strong, he's nearly knocking me over and he doesn't even know he's doing it. I'm sure he doesn't mean it though.'

Lucas Lion wondered again why some animals were afraid of him and some weren't. He thought it was peculiar and he decided to find out.

Placing one big paw in front of the other he shook his fine mane. Lucas stopped to look down at the tortoise who was moving gradually at a listless pace along the floor.

to get a closer look at the big Lion.

'Are animals afraid of me?' Lucas Lion asked bluntly.

'Well,' said the quiet Tobey, considering his answer, 'Sometimes.'

'Why?' asked Lucas Lion, bemused.

'Well, your roar is so loud and you're so big and strong. It can be quite frightening for some of the animals, especially the little ones.'

'Oh,' said Lucas Lion, surprised at the answer. 'Are you afraid of me?'

'Uh huh.' Tobey Tortoise nodded his head very slowly.

around the room. He was standing all on his own.

He realised that, even though he was big and strong and powerful and everyone looked up to him, he was still all on his own!

What could he do to change the situation?
He thought and thought and thought. Then, after
much consideration, he decided that he would be
different.

Lucas Lion lifted a massive paw and tapped at his eyebrow.

And then he thought and thought and thought some more. His feelings confused him.

Then, suddenly, his head popped up and he realized a very important fact. He was perfect just as he was.

'Why should I change who I am?' he wondered.

I smile more when I'm roaring the other animals won't be so afraid.' Lucas Lion let out a loud roar, once more blasting a wave of hot breeze around the room.

The other animals stopped and looked at him with wide, scared eyes.

And do you know what?

The other animals, big and small, smiled right back.

Lucas realized that how we feel inside might not always be the same as how we act or appear to others.

Lucas Lion!' and she straightened her leaves a little more and stretched.

How are you feeling today?

On the number scale where would you put your feelings of bravery right now?

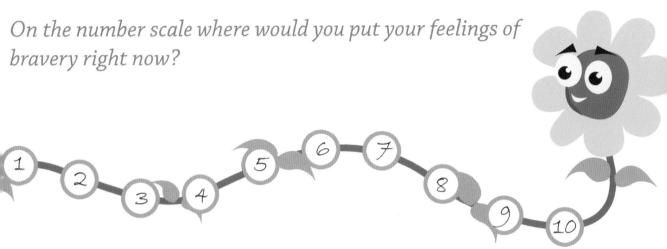

Let's see if we can make that number smaller!

Let's go on a Bravery Holiday with Lucas!

Take a deep breath in ….. hold it in and anything that doesn't feel so brave today …. let it all go in one big breath.

Try this three times. Breathe in bravery…

..and any little thing that might be stuck inside ….. let it all go!

little Tapping with Lucas!

Make a list of all the brave words you know and using each Tapping point ...

let's Tap together - Using the tips of your first two fingers gently tap on each Tapping point.

We can help Lucas to feel brave. Here's a list of words to help you.....

Choose one word for each tapping point ..... or look up some of your own words.

Brave

Strong

Powerful

Amazing

Courageous

Confident

Heroic

Dashing

Thoughtful

Wonderful

Secure

Incredible

Fearless

Lion hearted

Unafraid

Profound

Different

Special

Me

Let's Tap with Lucas! I am .....

1 Top Of Head
2. Inner Eyebrow
3. Outer Eyebrow
4. Under Eye
5. Under Nose
6. Groove Of Chin
7. Collar Bone
8. Under the Arm
9. Thumb Nail
10. Index Finger
11. Middle Finger
12. Ring Finger Nail
13. Baby Finger Nail
14. Sword of Hand

Your Tapping Points

Now check the number scale and see what number you have chosen? Is it higher? Why not do it again and see if you can make that number smaller...

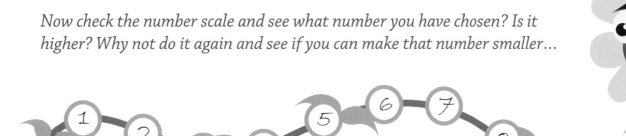

Different & Special

by Sarah Gilbert

I don't always feel brave!

Sometimes I can't even wave!

But I am strong and I am tall,

I'm different and I'm special,

That's all!

look out for verse three in the story of Tobey Tortoise!

Printed in Great Britain
by Amazon

37215751R00021